I'll Be There For You

Paul Taylor

Written by Paul Taylor   **Harbor House Publishing**   Illustrated by Jeric Tan

I'll Be There For You
© 2022 Paul Taylor

ISBN: 9798795420950

Harbor House Publishing, LLC | www.harborhousepublishing.com
Smyrna, Tennessee

Harbor House Publishing

To **Abby**, the love of my life.

You inspire me each day by
your shining example of
what it means to be there
for others, no matter what.

If I want you or need you, what will you do?

I will come right there to you.
I'll be there for you.

What if I find both
my socks, but I
can't find my shoes?

I will come right
there to you.
I'll be there for you.

What if I fall off my scooter, and I get a boo-boo?

I will come right there to you. I'll be there for you.

What if **I**'m making cool crafts, and **I** run out of glue?

I will come right there to you.
I'll be there for you.

What if I can't reach the spices I need for my stew?

I will come right there to you.
I'll be there for you.

What if the lemurs distract me, and I get lost in the zoo?

I will come right there to you. I'll be there for you.

What if I'm solving a mystery but can't find the next clue?

I will come right there to you. I'll be there for you.

What if my band has a concert, and I'm playing the kazoo?

I will come right there to you.
I'll be there for you.

What if I'm cornered by ninjas, but I don't know kung-fu?

I will come right there to you. I'll be there for you.

What if I need a teddy bear for my sleep, yummy food for my tummy, a hug for my hurts, a tissue when my nose gets runny,

a kiss on my cheek,
a towel for my bath,
rides to my school,
and help with
my math?

Can you do all
those things?
What will you do?

I'll be there for you.
I love you – I do.

The End!

For Parents

Many kids in our world don't have someone in their life who they trust will be there for them, no matter what.

Please consider being a family that fosters. A family that says,

"I'll be there for you. I love you - I do."

Made in the USA
Columbia, SC
14 March 2022

57630187R00015